Good Job,
Kanani

by Lisa Yee

★ American Girl®

For Roger and Pat

*Special thanks to Jennifer Hirsch for helping bring
Kanani's stories to life*

Published by American Girl Publishing, Inc.
Copyright © 2011 by American Girl, LLC

Printed in China
11 12 13 14 15 16 17 LEO 10 9 8 7 6 5 4 3 2 1

Illustrations by Sarah Davis

Questions or comments? Call 1-800-845-0005, visit our Web site at americangirl.com,
or write to Customer Service, American Girl, 8400 Fairway Place, Middleton, WI 53562-0497.

This book is a work of fiction. Any similarity to real persons, living or dead, is coincidental
and not intended by American Girl. References to real events, people, or places are used
fictitiously. Other names, characters, places, and incidents are the products of imagination.

Cataloging-in-Publication Data available from the Library of Congress.

Contents

Kanani Akina lives in Hawai'i, on the island of Kaua'i (kuh-WAH-ee), so you will see some Hawaiian words in this book. If you can't tell what a word means from reading the story, you can turn to the Glossary of Hawaiian Words on page 105. It will tell you what the word means and how to pronounce it.

Kanani Akina's name is pronounced like this: kuh-NAH-nee ah-KEE-nuh.

Kanani Akina looked out over the long line, a mix of regular customers and new ones. No one seemed to mind the wait. Everyone in Waipuna knew that for the best shave ice, you went to Akina's Shave Ice and Sweet Treats. Kanani's family had owned it for generations; as the sign outside the weathered green building said, it was "sorta famous."

Heads turned and eyes widened as each customer was handed a huge cone of powdery ice laced with delectable homemade syrups such as passion fruit, pineapple, and mango. In all, there were over fifty flavors to choose from.

"This is our newest shave-ice flavor," Kanani announced, pointing up at the wall where choices were painted on pieces of driftwood. "It's called Rachel's Big Apple!"

Two weeks ago, Kanani's cousin, Rachel Sutton, was at Akina's helping to greet customers. Now she was back in New York City. Kanani felt a tug on her heart when she thought about her cousin. The month they had spent together had started off a bit rocky, but as time went by, they had grown closer than either would have ever guessed possible.

It was Malana that brought us together, Kanani reflected. She glanced over at a woman who was

1

reading a framed news story from *The Daily Breeze* that was mounted on the wall. The article told of the monk seal pup that had become entangled in a net and almost died. It went on to report about the two girls—Kanani and Rachel—who found the seal and called the Hawaiian Monk Seal Foundation, and how the seal had been saved. Accompanying the story were photos that Kanani herself had taken of the seal-rescue operation.

"That poor seal," the woman said, taking a spoonful of shave ice. "I hope it survives."

"The seal's been doing well," Kanani assured her. "We call her Malana, and she's thriving."

"Well, that's a relief. I had no idea that seals were endangered."

"Most seals aren't, but the Hawaiian monk seal is," Kanani replied. "There are only about eleven hundred left in the whole world, and they live only in Hawai'i."

Kanani was glad her mother had hung the article on the wall. *If only,* she thought, *there was a way to let more people know about the monk seals.*

A man with a serious sunburn was next in line. "Hmmm," he mused. "Everything here looks so good. What do you think I should get?"

"You can't go wrong with a shave ice," Kanani told him. "But if you like bakery treats, today's specials include macadamia-nut shortbread cookies dipped in milk chocolate, and mini banana cupcakes topped with coconut buttercream frosting. Plus, there's our mochi." She motioned to the smooth balls of pastel-colored, sweet and sticky rice.

The man chuckled. "Now I'm more undecided than ever. You make everything sound wonderful!"

Kanani beamed. She loved talking to customers and answering their questions. The look on their faces when they tried the treats was her reward. The store had a motto: "Smiles guaranteed or your money back," and in the history of Akina's, no customers had ever asked for their money back.

When Kanani was done helping out at the store, she headed home to do her chores. Along the way she stopped to take photos of a neighbor's colorful clothesline, of some kids playing ball, and of an elderly neighbor, Mr. Lee, who was sitting in his living room looking out the window. As she raised her camera to snap his picture, he grinned and waved, as if delighted by the unexpected attention.

Kanani's home was a small peach-colored house. The sweet-smelling gardenia bush in front always greeted her—as did Barksee, her bright-eyed mutt. Walking around the house to the backyard, Kanani spotted her little black-and-white goat hiding behind the mango tree.

"Mochi, come here!" she called out. "What trouble have you gotten into today?" Mochi the goat peeked out from behind the tree, looking as innocent as could be. She had a shred of paper stuck to her face, and at her feet were the remains of a cereal box.

"Ahem! Looks like someone's been in the trash again," Kanani said, trying to sound stern but not succeeding. "Has anyone seen Jinx?"

As if on cue, a loud crowing pierced the air. Jinx the rooster was striking with metallic green and orange feathers, and the red crown on top of his head signaled to all who saw him that he was in charge. Kanani bowed. "Hello, your majesty," she said as he strutted past her. Though he was not as friendly as Barksee and Mochi, Kanani adored him. She had gotten Jinx when he was just a tiny chick, and she felt proud of what a handsome, regal bird he had become.

With pets following her, Kanani filled a pitcher with water and poured it into the three bowls lined up on the back porch. Just as she was about to head inside, she remembered another one of her chores.

"Junk mail, junk mail, junk mail," she said impatiently as she emptied the big metal mailbox. Her friends Celina and Seth were waiting for her at the beach. Celina's older brother, Seth, was the best surfer in Waipuna. He had offered to take the girls surfing, and Kanani was eager to get to the beach. But her eyes grew wide when she noticed a small box wedged in the back of the mailbox. Leaving the rest of the mail to be sorted on the kitchen table, she rushed to her room with Barksee at her heels. Plopping down on her bed, Kanani examined the brown-paper package. "It's from Rachel," she told Barksee. "See, it's postmarked New York."

Kanani shook the package and then quickly opened it. "Look!" she exclaimed. "It's a digital-photo frame!"

Rachel had already uploaded several pictures, and Barksee let out an appreciative woof as Kanani pored over the shots—one of her cousin in front of the Statue of Liberty, and one of what had to be Rachel's new apartment. Her room looked sleek and sophisticated, like Rachel herself. Another photo was of Aunt Jodi, Rachel's mom, with her new husband, Paul, and Rachel in the middle. Kanani was pleased to see how happy they all looked.

Kanani was so engrossed, looking at the photos, she almost missed the postcard at the bottom of the box. It showed a giant apple with the New York skyline behind it. Rachel had written:

Aloha, Kanani!
    How's Malana? Do you ever see her? Is she getting big and fat? Are her scars healing?
    This digital frame is for your amazing photographs.
Love, Rachel
P.S. Say aloha to Celina for me and, yes, to Pika too.

Kanani smiled. Pika was an annoying boy who had a habit of showing up and inserting himself into every situation. She had to admit, though, that Pika had played an important role in helping save Malana when she was tangled in the net by keeping onlookers away until help arrived. Still, Kanani usually tried to avoid Pika and his smart-aleck comments.

She gave Barksee a hug. "Be good while I'm gone. I can't bring you because you can't surf. Actually, neither can I—that's why Seth is helping me." Quickly she pulled on her swimsuit and slipped a long-sleeved T-shirt over it to protect her arms from the sun. Then she grabbed her beach bag and set off down the road to Waipuna Beach.

Celina waved from the water and paddled in from the surf. Her wet black hair was slicked back. "I couldn't wait to get started," she said apologetically. "I hope you don't mind."

"No, of course not. Sorry I'm late," Kanani said.

"Are you ready to surf?" Seth asked, handing her a board. Seth was tall and tanned, and his wavy brown hair was flecked with blond. Teenage girls hung around the beach rental stand when he was working. His dream was to be a professional surfer.

"Let's go over this again," he said to Kanani as he began reviewing the five basic steps. "When you feel the momentum of your surfboard is faster than you're paddling, that's when you stand up . . ."

As Seth talked, Kanani recognized the pained smile he was wearing. It was the one he used when he tried to be patient with his beginning students. She could see Celina out on the ocean, standing on her surfboard and making it look easy.

"Kanani, you need to pay attention," said Seth.

"What? Oh, yeah," she said, turning back toward Seth. Everyone in Celina's family surfed—even her parents. Every now and then, Kanani's father would take out his board. But lately he had been so busy with the store, he seldom had time to go out on the water. Kanani remembered watching him ride the waves when she was younger and wanting to be just like him.

At last, when Seth pronounced her ready to surf, Kanani waded out and climbed onto her board.

"Isn't this fun?" Celina asked as she and Kanani paddled out side by side, lying on their surfboards and paddling with their arms.

"Sure," Kanani said, hoping that once she got better at surfing, it would be.

"Here comes a wave," Seth called out. "You both remember what to do, right?"

Kanani felt her heart race as the wave grew bigger. She glanced over at Celina, who was busy paddling, and tried to do the same. "Use your arms more," Celina called out. "Make big circles, like this!"

For a while Kanani kept up with her best friend. But when she tried to place her feet on the board as Seth had taught her, she felt off-balance, and before she knew it, Kanani was in the water. She surfaced in time to watch Celina standing with her arms stretched out, riding the wave in to shore.

"That was a good try," Celina said as they waited for the next wave. "If you got up a little faster, maybe that might help."

Kanani nodded, her heart pounding. There was so much to remember.

"Here comes another wave," Celina shouted. "Come on, Kanani, let's ride this one together!"

Side by side, the girls paddled as fast as they could. They both planted their feet on their boards and rose in unison. But instead of riding the wave into shore, Kanani lost her balance and fell backward into the water. When she surfaced, she could see Celina still standing on her surfboard in the distance.

Kanani sighed. If there was ever a competition for the most wipeouts, she'd win for sure. "Let's go get a shave ice," she called to Celina.

"Are you kidding?" Celina pointed to the wave break. "Look—there are still plenty of waves! You go on without me. I'll catch you later."

Before going back to Akina's, Kanani climbed over the rocks to 'Olino Cove to see if Malana might be hauled out at the secluded beach.

But the small beach *wasn't* secluded—a group

of people had gathered at the water's edge. Were they looking at a seal? Suddenly, Kanani spotted a familiar face.

"Come on, people! Give the seal some space," Pika was telling the bystanders.

Kanani rushed up to him. "It's getting awfully crowded here," she whispered, knowing seals could be scared by loud noises.

"I know," he grumbled. "The cove used to be a local secret, but now it seems like the whole world knows."

"And they're way too close to Malana," Kanani agreed. "Everyone, please stand back!" she called out. But the crowd didn't budge.

"We heard about the monk seal," said a man wearing binoculars. He motioned to his wife and two young children. "We're visiting the island, and this is something we didn't want to miss!"

"Can I pet the seal?" his little girl asked as she walked toward Malana.

"Oh no, no!" Kanani said quickly. "Please keep away from the seal—you don't want to scare her! Plus, if she's frightened, she might bite. But if you stand far enough back, you can take her picture." Kanani turned to Pika. "Can you go call the monk seal coordinator? I'll keep watch over Malana until the volunteers arrive."

As Pika took off, Kanani approached the small crowd and began tapping people on the shoulder and saying, "Excuse me, but could you please move back? This young seal really needs her rest and shouldn't be disturbed."

"Does this seal come here often?" a woman with oversized sunglasses asked.

Once Kanani began telling everyone about Malana, they were more than happy to cooperate. *People really do want to do the right thing,* Kanani realized; *they just don't know how.*

Kanani wished she had a way to let people know how they could help protect the seals. She had thought of printing up some posters about the seals and putting them up around Waipuna, so that people would know what to do—and what *not* to do—if they saw one. But Celina had told her that posters were quite expensive to have made. That had given Kanani another idea. And now, after seeing the crowd around Malana, she knew it was time to put her idea into action.

"Hey, just the person I was hoping to see!" Kanani's father called out when she entered the store. "Come with me to test out the new shave-ice cart. Would Celina like to come, too?"

"She's still surfing," Kanani told him. "But I can't wait to try it out!"

It was true. She was excited about the cart. In fact, she had some plans of her own for it. All she had to do was convince her dad to go along with her.

Kanani and her father got into his truck and drove the few blocks to the pier, hauling the shave-ice cart behind them. The bright pink cart with its thatched roof made quite a sight being towed down Koa Street behind the old red pickup, and when they passed people they knew, the other drivers honked and waved. At the pier, Mr. Akina parked, unhooked the cart, and rolled it into position near the beach.

Mr. Akina opened a cooler, lifted a block of ice onto the machine, and turned it on. Soft particles of ice as light as snowflakes flew off, ready to be packed into a cone. Because the cart was small, they were limited to a dozen syrup flavors. Kanani had selected pineapple, passion fruit, strawberry, banana, lemon, mango, orange, honeydew, raspberry, coconut, grape, and of course, Rachel's Big Apple.

"Dad, guess what," Kanani said while she arranged the small flat wooden spoons, straws, and napkins. "Rachel sent me a digital frame—it's portable and can display hundreds of photos!"

"She knows how much your photographs mean to you," he said as he expertly packed a cone. Though they had been open for only a few minutes, several customers had already shown up.

Kanani nodded. "She asked about Malana on her postcard. Rachel loves the monk seals as much as I do. Don't you think that seals are totally adorable? And do you realize there are only eleven hundred left in the entire world?" Her voice rose higher. "Someone should do something to help them. If only someone could help tell everyone about the monk seals . . ."

Mr. Akina looked fondly at his daughter. "Kanani, is there some point you're trying to make?"

"Well," she said, choosing her words carefully, "I thought that maybe I could get some colorful posters printed telling people about the monk seals and how we can help them. I could put them up all over town. But since posters are sort of expensive, I was hoping that—well, that maybe—maybe I could use the shave-ice cart to raise the money. I'd work it myself, and I'm sure Celina would help, and we'd only use it when you weren't, and part of the sales could go toward the fund-raising, and—"

"Whoa!" Mr. Akina said, holding up his hands. "Running the shave-ice cart is a lot of responsibility."

Kanani's heart sank. When her dad used that lecturing tone, it usually meant he was going to say no. "Dad," she said quickly, "you know the Arts and Crafts Festival is in just a few weeks. You'll be so busy at the store, you'll need someone else to run the stand."

The Waipuna Arts and Crafts Festival was the most exciting weekend of the year. The Waipuna Surf Competition was held on the same weekend, and the Akinas could count on the store bustling with eager customers.

Mr. Akina smiled. "It's good to have ambition, but before you start raising money, you're going to have to have a goal. I need to see your business plan."

"My *what*?" Kanani asked.

"Your business plan. Figure out how many posters you're going to need, how you're going to make them, and how much it will cost to print them. Get me that information, and then, if you think you can handle the responsibility of working the shave-ice cart with Celina—"

Before her father could finish his sentence,

Kanani was jumping up and down and hugging him. He laughed and hugged her back.

"Excuse me?" Someone coughed. "Excuse me, I hate to interrupt this happy-happy fest, but can I get some service here?"

Kanani turned. "Sure, Pika, what flavor would you like?"

He looked at the syrups and then announced, "All of them."

"Yeah, right—only three flavors per cone, Pika," she said with a grin. Today not even a pest like Pika could dampen her spirits. She could hardly wait to tell Celina the great news.

"Do you want to come with me to Wiki Wiki Print Shop?" Kanani asked Celina the next day as they rested on the rocks after their surfing lesson. Surfing had gone a little better than the previous day, and Kanani hoped she was starting to get the hang of it.

"Now? But don't you want to surf some more, after we take a break?" Celina asked.

"Well, I've already changed out of my swim-suit—and I want to get started on my poster project,"

Kanani admitted. "But you can go ahead and surf some more if you want."

"Well, I'm not allowed to surf alone, but maybe Seth can come with me on his next break. Hey, look—" Celina pointed up at the sky. "Doesn't that cloud look just like a whale?"

Kanani looked up. "Yes—and that one there looks like a birthday cake," she said, pointing to another fluffy white cloud. She and Celina loved finding shapes in the clouds. It was a game they had played since they were little.

Kanani wondered if she was being disloyal not to stay and surf some more with Celina. *But Malana needs me, too,* she thought. *I have to be loyal to her as well.* She stood up to go. "See you tomorrow."

"*How* much?" Kanani tried not to let her shock show, but it was too late. She had asked Susan, the owner of Wiki Wiki, for a price quote, but she wasn't prepared for the answer. "*Six hundred dollars?*"

Susan shrugged. "If you reduce the size of the poster, the price will go down. And we could use less-expensive paper, too."

Kanani mulled it over. "Okay, how about if we

make the posters smaller and print seventy-five instead of a hundred?" She bit her nails as Susan punched new numbers into her calculator.

"Four hundred and fifty dollars?" Kanani's heart sank as she looked at the new price. That was still so much money! "The posters are to tell people how to help save the endanged Hawaiian monk seals," Kanani pointed out. "Is there any way I can get them done for less? What if we put the name of your print shop on the poster, so that everyone knows that Wiki Wiki Print Shop cares about the monk seals?"

Susan nodded slowly, and her dangling earrings swayed. "Well, that would be nice advertising for us, and trying to save the seals is a good cause. How about we print sixty posters at eighteen by twenty-four inches, and I'll charge you three hundred dollars even?"

That was a hundred and fifty dollars less. It still was an awful lot of money, but Kanani knew Susan's offer was a good one. The rest was up to her.

"It's a deal," she said, shaking Susan's hand. "I'll be back when I have the money!"

Kanani headed home with a spring in her step. But as she started thinking about what lay ahead, she began to slow down. *Three hundred dollars! How will I ever earn that much money?*

That night, over a dinner of grilled fish, rice, and cabbage, Kanani told her parents about how much the posters would cost. She watched her father carefully and tried to gauge his expression.

"I tell you what," he said. "You did your home-work as I asked. So, you can run the shave-ice cart in the afternoon. For every cone you sell, you can keep fifty cents to go toward the monk seal posters." Kanani sat up straight. "But you can't run the cart alone," her father cautioned.

"Celina will be with me," Kanani assured him.

"And you have to be finished by the time school starts. Agreed?"

"Agreed!" Kanani said, grinning.

As she ate, numbers bounced around in her head. To make three hundred dollars, she would have to sell six hundred cones of shave ice in less than thirty days. That was a lot of shave ice! Kanani imagined rows and rows of shave-ice cones in a rainbow of colors.

"Business at the store is already picking up.

I think this year's festival will be busier than ever," said Mrs. Akina, bringing Kanani out of her daydream.

All year Kanani looked forward to the Arts and Crafts Festival. She liked to spend hours going from booth to booth, talking to the artists and admiring their painted landscapes, handmade jewelry, unique pottery, photography, and crafts.

"I can't wait to see what Aunty Verna will have at the festival this year," Kanani said. Aunty Verna wasn't Kanani's real aunt, but on the island, close family friends were often called "Aunty" and "Uncle." Last year her parents had purchased one of Aunty Verna's elegant raku vases, with an iridescent blue sheen that made it look like it was glowing from within.

"Aunty Verna won't be able to show her pottery this year," Kanani's mother said gently. "Ever since her stroke, she hasn't been able to work the potter's wheel."

"But Aunty Verna always comes to the festival," said Kanani. "Can't she come just to look, even if she's not selling anything?"

Mrs. Akina shook her head. "I don't think so, Kanani. Just getting out of the house has become difficult for her."

Kanani felt a little ache in her heart at this

news. Aunty Verna always said that she looked forward to the festival all year, and she had attended
every festival since the very first one.

The Akinas purchased a new piece of art at the
festival each year to display in the store, which looked
a bit like a jumbled art gallery. Behind the counters
full of treats, the walls were crowded with paintings
and photographs, and a special display shelf held
delicate pieces like Aunty Verna's raku vase. The
tradition had been started the very first year of the
festival, when Kanani's father was a boy. Kanani's
parents had continued the tradition, and each year
Kanani couldn't wait to see what they selected out of
all the art being exhibited.

"The festival just won't be the same without
Aunty Verna," Kanani said wistfully. "I wonder what
art piece you'll buy this year."

"Well, this time we thought we'd do something
different," Mrs. Akina said. "You've been working so
hard at the store and it hasn't gone unnoticed. Plus,
you're taking on a big responsibility by raising money
to help the monk seals."

"So," her father continued, "instead of your
mother and me deciding what to get, we thought
maybe you'd like to make the selection this year."

Kanani looked up, her eyes shining. "Really? Me?" It was an honor to be asked to carry on the Akina tradition.

Her parents smiled. "That is, if you would like to," said Mr. Akina.

"Shopping is a serious responsibility, you know," said her mother with a wink.

Kanani beamed. She couldn't wait to tell Celina all the news!

The next day, Kanani and Celina met at the lifeguard stand at Waipuna Beach after lunch. There would just be time for a quick snorkel before Seth took them out surfing.

"Wow, Kanani—that's pretty cool," Celina said as she toyed with the strap on her snorkeling gear. "You get to pick the artwork at the festival, *and* your dad agreed to let you use the shave-ice cart to raise money?"

Kanani felt giddy as they walked toward the water. "That's right! Isn't it great? Hey—do you remember when we had that lemonade stand?"

"Yes, and we sold cookies, too," Celina recalled. "It was so much fun. How old were we? Six or seven?"

"I think we were in first grade," Kanani said.

"Remember when we forgot to add sugar to one of the pitchers of lemonade?"

"And Mr. and Mrs. Lee were too kind to tell us how sour it tasted," Kanani said. "Do you remember who finally told us?"

"*Pika!*" Celina shrieked.

"Yes," Kanani cried. "He spit out the lemonade and then flung himself to the ground and pretended we had killed him!"

Both girls dissolved into laughter. Kanani felt a delicious shiver of anticipation. Working at the shave-ice stand with Celina was going to be such a blast!

"So, when do we start selling shave ice?" Celina asked. "You know I help at the restaurant during the lunch shift." Celina's family owned the Waipuna Kitchen, a popular lunch spot.

"Yes, and I help out at Akina's in the morning," said Kanani. "Let's start tomorrow, right after you're done."

"Sure," Celina said. "Shave-ice cart, then surfing. Sounds like a plan. Come on, let's snorkel."

The girls put on their masks and dove into the clear blue water. Kanani felt exhilarated as she swam through schools of colorful fish. There was always something fascinating to see, like a turtle swimming gracefully through the shallow water or an octopus hiding in a rock crevice. *What a perfect way to spend a summer afternoon with my best friend,* thought Kanani. Turning to face Celina under the water, Kanani gave her a *shaka*—a fist with her thumb and pinky raised, which meant, "everything's good!"

The following day, under Mr. Akina's watchful eye, the girls were in business. Kanani had made a sign that read, "Fifty cents of every shave ice sold helps save the Hawaiian monk seal." She had included a photo of Malana tangled in the net and a larger shot of a healthy Malana at 'Olino Cove.

It took a while to get used to the cart. At Akina's everything was in its proper place, and Kanani could practically pour the syrups with her eyes closed. But here, the bottles were different and there was less space, so the girls kept bumping into each other. After the first hour, they fell into a steady rhythm, with Kanani in charge of the shave ice and Celina taking the money and making change.

Soon customers found their way to the cart. Many of Akina's regulars were pleased to be able to get their shave ice so close to the beach. Every so often, Kanani peeked into the tin money box where she was saving her share of the sales. Her heart raced when she saw it start to fill up. It was only the first day, and already they had made twelve dollars and fifty cents!

"How much longer?" Celina asked.

"How much longer until what?"

"How much longer until we surf?" Celina asked.

"Oh, right. Let's just sell a couple more, and then we can surf."

Celina's face lit up. "You know what, Kanani? By the time school starts, you and I are going to be awesome surfers!" she exclaimed. "I can already tell."

"Okay, when you're on the water and the surf starts to feel like it's flowing faster than you can paddle, that's the time to stand," Seth explained once more. "Then you quickly push up and extend your arms like this, keeping your weight balanced with a slight lean forward."

Kanani nodded. Celina was already in the water surfing. In the distance Kanani spotted a trio of boys heading toward them and dragging their boogie boards in the sand.

Seth continued, "Your feet should be planted firmly on the board, here and here." Kanani stood on her board and put her feet where Seth showed her. It was easy—because her surfboard wasn't anywhere near the water; they were still on the beach. "Good," he said. "Now don't stand up straight. Instead, crouch like this. Focus on keeping your weight on the center of the board, and just go with it!"

Everything he said tumbled around and around in Kanani's head. She wondered if Seth could tell that she was having a hard time keeping all the details straight. She watched Celina standing on her board, making it look so easy.

As Kanani and Seth carried their boards to the water, someone yelled, "Hey, look—it's Jill Sakamoto!"

Kanani turned to see Pika snickering with his friends Ryan and Keala. Jill Sakamoto was from Waipuna and had won major surf competitions. She had even been on the cover of *Surfin'* magazine.

"Oops. Sorry," Pika said as he tossed his blue boogie board in the water. "I mistook you for someone who's coordinated."

"Go away, Pika," Kanani bristled. Pika's teasing

smarted. When she and Celina had decided to take up surfing, Kanani was convinced that she'd love it and be good at it, like her dad. But now that she was actually trying it, she wasn't so sure. She was a strong swimmer and pretty good at bodysurfing, and she did perfectly well on a stand-up paddleboard. So why couldn't she surf?

"Kanani, stay focused!" Seth shouted as they headed out toward the waves.

Celina beamed and waved when Kanani paddled up to her. As they sat on their boards, she confided, "I'm so happy you're here! While you and Seth were back there on the beach, for a minute I thought maybe you were going to change your mind about coming out. Isn't that silly?"

Kanani gave her friend a weak smile. "Well, here I am! Ready to fall off my board and into the Pacific Ocean," she joked.

"You're getting better," Celina said encouragingly. "All you need is more practice. Don't worry. We'll put in more time, and you'll be an expert surfer soon!"

Kanani awoke to the sound of crowing. Quickly she got dressed, wishing she could skip the whole morning and go straight to selling shave ice at the pier with Celina. In four shifts they had earned nearly fifty dollars, and Kanani felt they were on a roll.

"Good morning," her mother said as Kanani sat down at the kitchen table. She set a plate of white rice topped with fried Spam and scrambled eggs in front of Kanani, who always had a big appetite in the morning.

"You and Celina have been doing a great job with the shave-ice cart," her father said as Kanani dug into her breakfast. "I've been hearing from customers how professional you are."

Kanani beamed. "Thanks, Dad. But I wish we could spend more time raising money. Two hours a day isn't enough, but Celina wants to surf every afternoon."

"Two hours is plenty of time," her mother replied. "Besides, you're helping at the store in the mornings, and Celina helps at Waipuna Kitchen at lunch. You girls need time to go out and have fun."

"Speaking of fun, how's the surfing been?" Mr. Akina asked as he refilled his coffee mug. "I've got to find some time to get out on the water. Maybe after the festival, when things have quieted down."

Kanani swallowed a bite of eggs. "It's fine," she said. "Celina's really, really good."

"It runs in her family," Mr. Akina noted. "I hear Seth has a good shot at getting sponsored."

Kanani nodded. To get a sponsor meant that you were a professional surfer, and the best pros traveled to surfing competitions all over the world. Ever since Jill Sakamoto had gone pro, everyone in Waipuna wondered who among them would be next. Kanani knew for sure who it *wouldn't* be—her.

"Aloha and welcome to Akina's," Kanani called out, and she smiled brightly when she saw a familiar figure in the doorway. "Tutu Lani!" She hurried over to help the elderly woman into the store.

As always, Tutu Lani wore her gray hair in a stylish bun held with a sea turtle comb. Her bright yellow *mu'umu'u* also had a turtle pattern.

"Aloha, keiki!" she answered. Kanani knew *keiki* meant child in Hawaiian. "Can you bring me a chair?"

"Of course!" Kanani said, rushing to the back room to fetch one.

"Ah, *mahalo*," the old woman said as she eased herself into the chair and let out a contented sigh. "These legs aren't what they used to be."

"I haven't seen you in here for a while," Kanani noted. She handed Tutu Lani a cold orange soda pop.

"Yes, it's getting harder for me to get around," Tutu Lani confessed. "I had to drop off some fresh leis for Mr. Cotzee at Island Gifts. Once I rest up, would you mind walking an old lady home?"

"I would love to!" Kanani said, and her mother smiled her approval.

As the two slowly made their way up the winding red dirt road, Tutu Lani stopped to rest several times. When they came around the bend, they heard a loud, low whistle. It was Mr. Lee, an old man with a nearly bald head, waving from his usual spot at his living room window.

"I see you have a chaperone!" he called out to Tutu Lani.

"Yes, this young lady is helping me home," she said as Kanani waved back. "How have you been?"

Mr. Lee shrugged. "These days I'm slower than a snail on a Sunday."

Just then, his wife stepped outside. Mrs. Lee was a tiny woman with streaks of white in her gray hair. "His new walker is coming this week. Not exactly like the old days, when the two of us ran around Waipuna and stirred up trouble," she said, giving Kanani a wink. "Anything new in town?"

"Malana, the monk seal pup, has been visiting 'Olino Cove quite a bit," Kanani said.

"Yes, yes," said Mrs. Lee. "The little seal! We read about her in the *Daily Breeze*. I said to my husband, 'Look! It's our own Kanani and Pika who helped save the seal.' And you took the photos yourself, right, Kanani?"

Kanani blushed and nodded.

"We loved your photos!" Mr. Lee yelled.

"Well, Mr. Lee, when that new walker comes, you just keep to the speed limit," Tutu Lani called back, laughing. "At the rate I walk, we won't be home for three days, so we'd best be moving along now."

By the time they reached Tutu Lani's little blue cottage nestled in a fragrant garden of flowers, Tutu Lani was exhausted.

"Are you all right?" Kanani asked as she helped Tutu Lani up the creaky porch stairs and into the worn wooden rocking chair.

Tutu Lani waved her hand in the air. "I'm fine," she insisted. "Just old! Mr. Cotzee says that instead of me bringing my leis to him, he'll find someone to pick them up from my house."

Kanani considered how long it had taken Tutu Lani to walk home. Mr. Cotzee was probably right, she reflected, as she watched Sue, Tutu Lani's chicken, scratching at the ground. With her glossy golden feathers against the green grass, Sue looked as if she were posing for a portrait. Kanani pulled her camera from her pocket and quickly snapped some photos of the chicken.

After telling Tutu Lani good-bye, Kanani headed back into town. Maybe she could join Celina for lunch before they started their shave-ice shift. But when she arrived at Waipuna Kitchen, Celina wasn't there.

"She wanted to surf this morning. Since the restaurant's pretty quiet on Wednesdays, I told her she could skip the lunch shift," said Celina's mother. "But now that you're here, how about a bowl of saimin?"

Kanani realized that she did feel a little hungry. She quickly finished the bowl of noodles, and then hurried out to the beach to find Celina.

As she approached the far end of the beach, Kanani trained her camera lens out on the water. Two figures came into focus. Celina was surfing with

another girl who looked about their age, but Kanani
didn't recognize her. Stepping carefully around a large
sea turtle basking on the sand, Kanani looked up just
in time to see Celina and the other girl catch a large
wave. Like mirror images of each other, both girls rose
on their boards, stood, and rode the wave with perfect
balance and poise. Kanani sighed and wondered how
it would feel to be good at something like that.

When Celina caught sight of Kanani, she waved
and paddled in to shore. "Did you see us?" she gushed.
"Wasn't that a smooth ride?" Kanani nodded, eyeing
the other girl. "Oops, where are my manners? Kanani,
this is Jo—she's visiting from the Big Island for the
Arts and Crafts Festival. Her father's an exhibitor,"
said Celina. "Jo, this is Kanani. She's the one I told you
about. Come on out, Kanani—the waves are great!"

"The waves really are great," Jo echoed. "We've
been having a blast. Grab your board and join us!"

"Maybe after my shave-ice shift, I will." Kanani
tried to ignore a twinge of jealousy in her stomach.

"Just one more wave, okay, Kanani? Then I'll
come join you at the shave-ice cart," said Celina, and
without waiting for an answer, she and Jo ran back
into the water and hopped onto their surfboards.

That afternoon business was slow. Kanani felt

antsy, but Celina didn't seem to mind. She chattered happily. "Jo's going to enter the surfing competition. This is her fourth tournament already, and she's only twelve! Did you see her out there? She's a great surfer, don't you think?"

Kanani nodded. She was busy counting the cash box again. They had made only nine dollars. She sighed. "Maybe we should close up early today."

"Great idea," said Celina. "Let's hit the water. Jo's waiting for us!"

Kanani felt another funny twinge in her stomach. Maybe she hadn't had enough lunch. She turned to Celina, suddenly feeling awkward around her best friend. "Um, I'm feeling a little sick today, so I don't think I should," she stammered.

Concern washed over Celina's face. "What's the matter?"

"Well, I just started feeling weird not too long ago," Kanani said truthfully. "I'm sure it's nothing, but I should probably just take it easy today."

"Okay, you take care of yourself," Celina said as they closed up the stand. "I'll try to stop by your house later."

"Okay, see you later," Kanani said as Celina picked up her board and headed toward the surf.

Kanani slept fitfully, tossing and turning and kicking off her sheets. In her dreams she was surfing, but she kept wiping out over and over until—*thud.*

Ouch! Kanani sat up on the floor and rubbed her arm where she had fallen on it. She blinked at the bright sunlight streaming through her blinds. What time was it? She glanced at the clock. *What—eight o'clock?* It couldn't be!

Why hadn't Jinx woken her up?

Kanani rushed into her parents' bedroom, where her mother was asleep with a pillow over her head while her father snored.

"Wake up!" Kanani cried. "It's late."

Mrs. Akina yawned. "What time is it?" Her eyes opened wide when she saw the clock. "Honey," she said, shaking her husband, "we have to get up."

"I already took out the trash," he mumbled in his sleep.

"Dad, get up!" Kanani shouted. "We all overslept!"

As the Akinas rushed through breakfast, Kanani said, "I didn't hear Jinx this morning. Did either of you?"

"I never hear him," her father said. "I sleep like a log."

"A snoring log," Mrs. Akina teased. "But no, I didn't hear Jinx." She glanced out the window. "I suppose he's hiding somewhere."

Later that morning, as she refilled syrup bottles at the store, Kanani thought about Jinx. She couldn't remember a time when she hadn't awakened to his crow in the morning. It was one of those things she took for granted, like Celina being her best friend or Pika being a pest. She was used to Mochi getting into mischief, but up till now Jinx had been very predictable, even when he was being difficult.

Just when she was about to head home a little early to check on him, Celina came into the store with Jo.

"Feeling better?" Celina asked.

"I'm not sick," Kanani said, confused.

"But yesterday you said you weren't feeling well."

"Oh . . . oh, well, that was yesterday," Kanani quickly answered. "I'm fine now." She glanced at Jo. She was a little taller than Kanani and very tanned. Her copper-colored hair was short, and she was quite pretty, especially her emerald green eyes.

"I thought you were going to come by after surfing yesterday," Kanani said to Celina.

"I was," Celina said as she peered into the baked-goods case. "But the waves were so good, we stayed out much longer than we planned, and then we needed to get a bite to eat, and I wanted to show Jo around town." She glanced up. "Are you mad?"

Kanani forced herself to smile. "Of course not." She turned to Jo. "Do you like Waipuna?"

Jo nodded. "Your beach is terrific. I can't wait until the surfing competition."

"Jo's entering the junior girls' division," Celina said proudly. "She's an awesome surfer. Jo, remember that last wave? You nailed it! Oh, Kanani, you should have seen her out there!"

Kanani felt a rush of jealousy start to bubble up but quickly squelched it. Celina really seemed to enjoy Jo's company—and why not? They had so much in common. "Jo," she said, "Celina and I are running the shave-ice cart this afternoon. The money we make is going to help the monk seals. You should come by."

When Kanani caught Jo and Celina glancing at each other, her stomach fluttered. Why were they looking at each other like that? Had they talked about something when she wasn't around? Had they been talking about her?

"Well," Celina replied, "the surf conditions are almost perfect, and I promised Jo that I'd surf with her. But of course, I'll be at the shave-ice cart," she added. "You know I will."

"Sure, okay." Kanani's stomach fluttered again. "I'll see you soon," she said, waving good-bye as Celina and Jo left the store together.

The rest of the morning seemed to drag. At lunchtime, Kanani ran all the way home. She kicked off her shoes and burst into the house, startling Barksee. "Have you seen Jinx?" she asked. Barksee cocked his head and looked at her with soft brown eyes. "Come on, let's check the yard."

Kanani ran around the backyard calling, "Jinx? Jinx, where are you?" as Mochi and Barksee trotted after her. But the rooster was nowhere to be found. "Where could he be?" she asked Barksee. The dog didn't answer, but Kanani reached down and hugged him and didn't let go for a long time.

That afternoon both girls were quieter than usual at the shave-ice cart. As a contented customer strolled away with his rainbow shave ice, Celina asked Kanani, "What's the matter?"

39

"I think Jinx has run away," Kanani said glumly.

"I'm sure he'll turn up," Celina assured her. "Just wait until dinnertime. Maybe you can put out something special to tempt him to come back. You know how much he likes to eat."

"That's a good idea," Kanani said as she wiped off the syrup bottle with a wet rag. Celina knew Jinx pretty well. Kanani thought of all the fun they had had playing with him when he was a cute, fluffy little chick, and watching him grow up into a handsome— and rather conceited—rooster.

"Say," said Celina cautiously, "would you mind if we close up the shave-ice cart a little early? The waves have been great, and that way we can get some more surfing in. Plus, we already made seventeen dollars today!"

Kanani was caught off guard. One minute Celina was so understanding about Jinx, and the next she wanted to ditch the fund-raising and go surfing.

"Well, I would sort of rather stay and sell more shave ice," Kanani admitted. "But if you want to leave early, go ahead."

"Really?" Celina studied Kanani's face. "Are you sure? Because if you don't want me to go, then I won't."

Kanani was taken aback by how quickly Celina warmed to her offer, but she tried not to show it. What she really wanted to say was, "Please stay," but instead Kanani heard herself saying, "No, no, it's fine. Really. You go."

"All right then, I'll see you at the beach. I told Jo you wouldn't mind!"

As Kanani watched her run down to the beach, she thought, *Celina discussed with Jo the idea of leaving her shift early to go surfing?* She wondered whether Celina preferred Jo's company to hers. Kanani gazed across the beach to the water, squinting in the bright sunlight. She could see Celina and Jo paddling out to the waves together. Even though she knew that Celina was her best friend, Kanani suddenly felt very alone.

"Aren't you supposed to smile?"

Kanani whipped around. Pika was standing there holding his boogie board. His thick black hair looked lopsided. At school he always boasted that he cut it himself, and Kanani believed him. "Excuse me?" she asked, annoyed. Being alone was better than being bugged by Pika.

"Aren't you supposed to smile when you have a customer?" Pika held his boogie board over his head, shading his face from the sun.

Kanani put on a huge fake grin and said through gritted teeth, "How may I help you, sir?"

"Hmmm . . ." Pika glanced at the shave-ice flavors. "How about lime?"

"You know we don't have that here."

"Well, I was in the mood for something green, but if you're too grumpy to help me, then I think I'll take off. Bye, Miss Grumpus!"

Kanani shook her head. She knew that *Pika* meant "rock" or "stone" in Hawaiian, but to her it just meant "pest."

After twenty more minutes with no customers, Kanani closed up the shave-ice cart and walked slowly toward the surf break. Even from a distance, she could see Jo at ease on the water and in total control of her surfboard. She and Celina were having a great time. What was the point of joining them?

Kanani had turned to go home when she heard Pika call her name. "So, whatcha waiting for?" he asked as he put his boogie board into the water. "Are you surfing or not?"

"I'm surfing," Kanani hissed at him. If Pika knew that she was scared to surf, he'd never let her live it down.

"The surf's that way," Pika said, pointing to the

wave break near Celina and Jo.

Reluctantly, Kanani got a board from the surf shack and paddled away from the shore.

"Hey, Kanani!" Seth called out. He was sitting on his board as Celina and Jo surfed. "We've saved some of the best waves for you."

"Look!" Celina shouted. She pointed to a huge wave building in the distance.

Kanani felt her stomach turn over. Should she tell Celina how she felt?

Seth locked eyes with Kanani. "Are you ready?" he asked. She gulped and nodded. "Just remember not to tense up, and you'll do great," he said as he turned his board and began paddling rapidly toward the shore.

Don't tense up. Don't tense up. Don't tense up, Kanani reminded herself as she turned and paddled ahead of the wave. When the wave was close, she crouched and then began to stand. She made sure her feet were in the proper position as the wave began to carry the board in a whoosh. *Don't tense up. Don't tense up. Don't tense up.* Kanani felt the power of the wave beneath her as she rose and put her arms out for balance. The water carried her swiftly forward. She was nailing the ride!

Feeling confident, Kanani turned to look at Celina and Jo. She felt her foot slip, and suddenly she was in the water, churning and turning under the wave. As she swam upward, the surging wave knocked her down again and again. In a panic, she swallowed a gulp of water. Struggling for air, she finally managed to break through to the surface.

Kanani blinked. The sunlight hurt her eyes. The water around her was calm and glistening blue, as if there had never been a monster wave. Nearby, Celina and Jo were sitting astride their boards. Kanani gasped for air as she swam to her board. Instantly, Celina was next to her. "Are you okay?" Celina asked as Kanani clung to her surfboard. Jo looked worried.

"I'm fine," Kanani snapped. "Leave me alone." She was glad that she was in the water so that Celina couldn't tell she was crying. As she paddled in to shore, Kanani could hear Celina calling her, but she just kept paddling.

Kanani picked up Barksee's leash from its hook on the porch. "Come on, boy," she called. "Let's go for a walk." Barksee wagged his tail and hurried up to her. Mochi followed him. "Mochi, you be good," she said, giving the little goat a hug and a scratch behind the ears. "I'll play with you when we get back," she promised. "I know it gets lonely around here without Jinx. I miss him, too."

The sun was starting to set as Kanani and Barksee walked down the path to 'Olino Cove. Kanani wondered if Malana would be there. She hoped so— that would cheer her up.

As they made their way down the heavily wooded trail, Barksee suddenly pulled the leash out of Kanani's hand and ran ahead. "Barksee, come back!" Kanani called out. "You know you have to be on your leash—it's the law! Silly dog," she muttered as she climbed over the rocks that hid the entrance of the cove.

The sunset cast a golden glow on the water, and a feeling of calm washed over Kanani as she stepped out of the prickly brush and onto the soft, warm sand. "Barksee!" she called out. Suddenly she stopped. "Oh!"

"Hi, Kanani." Celina was petting Barksee,

who was slobbering all over her, licking her face and wagging his tail.

"Hello," Kanani said, looking around to see if Jo was there, too.

"I was hoping I'd see you here," Celina said. "How come you left this afternoon without even saying good-bye?"

"I just . . ." Kanani struggled to explain. "Well, you looked like you were having so much fun with that other girl, I didn't think anyone would notice if I left."

"She has a name," Celina pointed out. "It's Jo, and she's really nice."

Kanani stiffened. "It must be a relief to have someone good to surf with."

"I never said that," Celina protested.

"Well, I've seen how much fun you have surfing with her."

"I do have fun—is there something wrong with that?" Celina asked, sounding defensive.

"No, not at all," Kanani said. "If you consider surfing with Jo fun, then be my guest, and don't mind me and my shave-ice cart. I don't want to take up any of your valuable surfing time."

Celina looked confused. "You're not mad at me

for some reason, are you?" she asked.

"Why should I be mad?" Kanani grasped for words. "I mean, we agreed we'd spend the summer raising money to help the monk seals, but all you seem to want to do is surf."

Celina hesitated. Then she took a deep breath and said in measured tones, "Kanani, I thought we agreed that this summer would be all about surfing."

"What?" Kanani shook her head. "I never said that."

"Yes, you did." Celina's voice began to rise. "Even before you helped rescue Malana, you knew that this summer was going to be the one where we took up surfing. I thought you really wanted to do this."

Kanani's face burned. Celina was right. When she had first suggested that they learn to surf, Kanani had been excited. She had pictured herself riding the biggest waves in Hawai'i . . . until she actually tried it. "I never agreed to surf all day long," she retorted.

"Well, I never agreed to spend my whole summer working," Celina shot back. "I help out at my parents' restaurant every day. Why would I want to work at a shave ice cart after that, when I could be catching waves?"

The girls stared at each other for the longest time, neither one saying anything.

Kanani felt a pain in her chest. "If that's how you feel, then fine," she said finally. Her eyes were wet with anger and hurt. "Have a good time surfing with Jo."

Celina stared at her, and then turned and left without a word. Kanani stood silently as the waves lapped around her ankles.

That night, Kanani logged onto her e-mail and sent a message to her cousin.

> Hey, Rachel,
>   Remember how you thought I loved surfing? Well, the truth is, I think I hate it. It feels awful to be so bad at something, when your best friend is so good at it. Celina and I had a huge fight. I feel like she's betrayed me.
>   And as if that's not bad enough, remember my rooster, Jinx? He's disappeared.
>   I miss you.
> Aloha,
> Kanani

"Where's Celina?" Mr. Akina asked as he unhooked the shave-ice cart from the pickup truck.

"Oh, she's busy," Kanani said, trying to sound lighthearted. She looked around, half expecting, half hoping, that Celina would show up. Yet ten minutes later, when the stand was open for business, there was still no sign of Celina.

"Kanani," said her father, "when we first discussed you selling shave ice, we agreed there would be two of you running the cart."

"I can do this by myself," Kanani assured him.

"I know how capable you are," he said. "But you need two people to run the cart. I'm sorry, Kanani, but you'll just have to wait until Celina gets here."

"But Dad—" Kanani protested.

"Kanani, we had an agreement," he said firmly.

"Yes, but . . ." Kanani wasn't sure what more to say. She didn't want to admit that Celina might not show up at all—or to explain why.

"But what?" her father asked patiently.

"Here I am! Sorry I'm late." Pika stood next to the cart with a cheerful smile.

Kanani and Mr. Akina both stared at him.

"Late for what?" Kanani asked, confused.

"Why are you looking at me like that?" Pika

asked. "Do I have a booger in my nose or something?"

"What are you doing here?" Kanani whispered.

"Girl, just go with the flow," he whispered back. "I'm helping!"

"But—"

"I know, I know, you said to be on time," Pika said loudly. "Well, I'm here, aren't I, so stop acting all weird." Pika turned to Kanani's father. "Hey, Mr. Akina, your hair looks good. Did you just get it cut?"

Kanani's father ran his hand through his hair. "Yes, as a matter of fact, I did. Okay, then, kids, I'll be back to check on things in about an hour."

Kanani looked at Pika. "I don't get it."

"So what else is new?" Pika flashed a cocky grin. "I was down at the beach and saw Celina with her surfboard." Kanani winced when she heard Celina's name. "When I came up here to get a shave ice, I overheard your dad saying you needed two people to run the cart. I put two and two together. You can stop looking so surprised; it's getting old."

Kanani stammered, "Well, thanks, I guess—" Before she could ask Pika if Celina was with Jo, a man and young boy appeared.

"Welcome to Akina's Shave Ice on the Beach. What can I get for you?" Pika asked.

"Strawberry and purple," the little boy shouted happily.

The rest of the shift flew by. Though Kanani hated to admit it, Pika was a good helper. Naturally talkative, he chatted with each customer and never tired of telling them about the monk seals and how he had saved a seal pup from certain death. Several times, Kanani had to remind him that she had been part of the rescue effort, too. Yet despite his annoying exaggerations, some customers were so enthralled with the story that they donated extra money for the posters.

When business finally slowed down, Kanani turned to him. "Pika, what are you doing here?"

"That's a dumb question," he answered. "What do you think I've been doing, knitting a sweater? I'm selling shave ice."

Kanani rolled her eyes. "Duh, I know *that*. But why? Why would you help me out?"

He shrugged. "This is not about you, so don't start getting all conceited. I'm helping the monk seals. You think you're the only one who cares about them?"

Kanani hid a smile. So Pika had a heart after all—he just kept it well hidden under a thick layer of obnoxiousness. "Thank you, Pika," she said.

"Whatever." He shaded his eyes. "How come you and Celina aren't friends anymore?"

Kanani felt her face flush. "We're still friends."

"Well, you two used to be like twins, but now Celina's always with that other girl. Is she your replacement or something?"

Kanani flinched. "People can have lots of friends, you know, Pika. Although you probably wouldn't know that."

There were a few minutes of silence.

"Well, I guess it's time for me to go," said Pika. He stepped down from the cart and picked up his boogie board.

Kanani hesitated. "Pika?"

"Yeah?"

"Will you be back tomorrow?"

Pika scowled. "Maybe you should say, 'Pika, will you be back, tomorrow . . . please.'"

Kanani sighed. "Pika, will you be back tomorrow . . . please?"

"Well," he said. "This is prime boogie board time, but yeah, since you're begging me, I guess so."

Kanani bristled. "I wasn't begging you."

"Do you want me here or not?" he asked.

"Yes. Please."

"All right then, sheesh. I'll do it, I'll do it!"

Kanani shook her head as he ran off. She counted the money in her cash box. They had made twenty-one dollars and fifty cents—the best shift so far. *Anything for the monk seals,* she reminded herself— *even spending afternoons with Pika the pest.*

Over the next week, Kanani fell into a comfortable routine with Pika at the shave-ice cart. "I got a postcard from Rachel," she told him one afternoon. "She says that they aren't allowed to have dogs in her apartment building, but her mom says she can get a bird."

"She should get two," said Pika. "One would be lonely by itself."

Kanani looked at him with interest. She hadn't thought of that.

"What about Jinx?" Pika asked as he poured bright orange syrup on a tower of shave ice. "Have you found him yet?"

Kanani shook her head. "My mom and I call and search for him every morning on our way to the store, but so far no luck. Mrs. Lee phoned this morning to say that she heard a rooster crowing near their house, but by the time we got there, it was gone."

"It might not even have been Jinx," Pika mused. He wiped off the syrup bottle. "Kaua'i has a lot of wild roosters."

Kanani knew he was right. It was not uncommon to see chickens along the road, in the woods, or even at the park.

"Maybe you can get another rooster," Pika suggested.

Kanani's eyes flashed with indignation. "Pika, you can't just swap out one rooster for another. Jinx is special! He's part of my family."

"Calm down," Pika mumbled. "I was just trying to be helpful. Sheesh!"

The two glared at each other until they heard someone call out, "Pika! Kanani!" A man wearing a monk seal T-shirt approached. It was Jim Robins from the Monk Seal Foundation. "Hey, I was just visiting Malana. She sure does love your hidden cove. Say, how goes the fund-raising?"

"It's going great," Pika chirped. "We're making tons of money!"

"Well, we've made more than a hundred dollars so far," Kanani said.

Jim looked impressed. "That's great news!

When you've got your poster design done, be sure to run it past Julia and me before they're printed, okay?"

Kanani nodded. "I will."

"Jim, would you like a shave ice?" Pika asked. He smiled politely.

"You know it," Jim answered. "I'll have my regular."

"That'll be ten dollars," Pika said as he turned on the shave-ice machine.

"Ten dollars?" Kanani and Jim said at the same time.

"Well, it's three dollars for an ordinary customer," Pika explained. "But because you're special, it's ten dollars for you. Plus, all the proceeds go to help protect the monk seals. You do want to help protect them, don't you?"

When Jim handed over a ten-dollar bill, Kanani couldn't help admiring Pika's nerve.

The walk up the red dirt road to Tutu Lani's house was one Kanani never tired of. The road was cool and shady, with tall ferns and thick mossy banks and huge trees covered with purple flowers. Partway up the hillside, some kids were playing at Wailua Falls.

Kanani remembered being scared of the rope swing when she was smaller. Celina had been fearless and had coaxed her into trying it. Celina had always been better at mastering physical challenges, Kanani realized. In fact, it was one of the things she had always admired about Celina—her athletic skill and daring. Kanani wondered if Celina was surfing with Jo right now.

As she made her way toward Tutu Lani's house, Kanani looked around for Jinx. What if he had gone exploring and gotten lost? Kanani recalled the time when she and Celina had tried to take Jinx for a walk, but instead he had taken them for a run—and it took them half an hour to catch him.

"Aloha, keiki!" Tutu Lani called from her front porch as Kanani came into her yard. A warm breeze drifted through Tutu Lani's lush tropical garden.

"Aloha," Kanani said, coming onto the porch. At the old woman's feet were baskets filled with flowers—purple orchids, pink plumeria, and fragrant tuberose. An open Styrofoam cooler held several finished leis.

Kanani handed Tutu Lani a small bag. "I brought you some macadamia-nut brittle."

"Ah, my favorite! Mahalo, Kanani, for thinking

of me," said Tutu Lani, opening the bag and taking a bite. "I was just working on my leis. Sit down and let's talk story."

Kanani knew that talking story was when you relaxed and shared whatever was on your mind. "Well," she began, "I'm selling shave ice to raise money to help protect the monk seals."

The old woman nodded. "Go on."

Before long, Kanani was telling Tutu Lani about her fight with Celina and how badly things had gone. "We haven't even spoken to each other in a whole week."

Tutu Lani was silent, but Kanani knew she was listening to every word. Earlier that summer, when Rachel had been visiting, it was Tutu Lani who had taught Kanani how to really listen.

"Keiki," the old woman finally said, "I have been a widow for nearly twenty years, and my son Nolan and his family moved to the mainland last year. I miss them every day. Now it's just me and Sue." Tutu Lani pointed to her chicken, who was sleeping at the far end of the porch. "And now that it's hard for me to get around, I sometimes feel all alone here."

Suddenly Kanani felt that her problems weren't

quite so big. At least she had her family right here in Waipuna. Maybe she couldn't surf, but at least her legs were strong and healthy.

"I'm not telling you this for pity," Tutu Lani continued. "I am telling you this because you and Celina are more than best friends—you are like sisters. Come with me."

Kanani followed Tutu Lani into her house. As she stood in the living room, she marveled at all the sea turtles Tutu Lani had collected. Some were made out of glass, some were carved out of stone. There were sea turtle pillows, sea turtle paintings, sea turtle ceramics, sea turtle vases, and even a large sea turtle stained-glass window.

"Look," Tutu Lani said, holding out a framed photo. Kanani expected to see a sea turtle but instead found herself staring at two pretty young Hawaiian girls. "That's me!" Tutu Lani exclaimed. "That girl with me, the one with the flower in her hair, that's my best friend, Lily. She lives in California now, but even though we are separated by the Pacific Ocean, we will always be friends for life."

Kanani wondered if she and Celina would be friends for life. She wondered if they were even still friends at all.

"Does Lily love turtles, too?" she asked as they returned to the porch.

"It was Lily who gave me the first *honu* in my collection. She appreciates honu, but she doesn't love them as I do." Tutu Lani smiled. "Lily collects owls." She lowered her voice and confided, "I wouldn't want all those big round eyes staring at me! But that doesn't bother Lily." Kanani giggled.

Tutu Lani grunted as she settled back into her chair. "It's funny, keiki—when you get older, your body starts playing tricks on you, like slowing down, when what I really want to do is speed up." She reached for a basket of flowers, and Kanani took one too, copying the old woman's smooth movements as together they strung the flowers into leis.

"Oh my, where has the afternoon gone?" Tutu Lani exclaimed. An hour had passed, and Kanani was surprised to see that the baskets were all empty and a pile of beautiful, fragrant leis now filled the cooler.

"You made a lot of leis! Oh, they're so pretty," Kanani said with admiration.

"*We* made a lot," Tutu Lani corrected her. "But I'm afraid they won't be quite as pretty tomorrow when Mr. Cotzee comes to get them. They really

should be refrigerated and sold when they're fresh."

Kanani jumped up. "What if I take the leis to Mr. Cotzee right now? I'm going back to Akina's anyway, and Island Gifts is just across the street."

Tutu Lani hesistated, but Kanani could tell she was thinking about it. "Keiki, the cooler is heavy."

"Not for me," Kanani insisted. She flexed an arm muscle to show Tutu Lani how strong she was, and then lifted the cooler. "See?"

"Well, if you're sure it is no bother—"

"It's no bother at all. I would be glad to do it."

Tutu Lani grasped Kanani's hands. "Mahalo, Kanani, for your help. Come again soon."

Kanani smiled. "I will," she promised.

As she walked back to town, the cooler did start to feel a little bit heavy—but Kanani realized that for the first time since she and Celina had argued, her heart felt light. It had been good to spend the afternoon with a dear friend and to feel needed.

"Are you going to pick up leis from Tutu Lani again today?" Mrs. Akina asked. Her rag made a squeaking sound as she wiped fingerprints off the baked-goods counter. It had been two days since Kanani's visit with Tutu Lani, and she and her mother were working the morning shift in the store.

Kanani nodded. "I'll go as soon as Pika and I are done selling shave ice this afternoon."

"Pika?" her mother said. "I thought it was Celina who was helping you."

Kanani hesitated. She couldn't bring herself to tell her mother that she and Celina weren't even speaking to each other. "Um—well, she's really into surfing lately, so Pika has been helping out instead," she said truthfully.

Mrs. Akina stopped cleaning the counter. "Is everything all right between the two of you?"

Kanani looked down and stared at the cookies through the sparkling clean glass. How could she explain what had happened, when she wasn't even sure herself?

"Well, Celina's got a new surfing friend who's much better at it than I am. I was probably just hold-ing her back anyway. And Pika—well, he's a great salesman, if you can believe that—" Kanani couldn't stop her eyes from welling up with tears.

Mrs. Akina set down her rag and folded her daughter into a hug. "I'm sorry to hear things are rocky between you and Celina. You two have been best friends for so long, it must feel strange to be growing apart."

Growing apart? Kanani's breath stopped for a moment in her chest. Was that what was happening to her and Celina?

"I—I miss her so much," Kanani sobbed into her mother's shoulder. "What if she just doesn't like me anymore?"

Mrs. Akina stroked Kanani's hair until her sobbing quieted. Then she spoke softly. "Trouble between friends can be very painful. Try to focus on other things," she urged.

"But I can't *help* thinking about it," Kanani said, wiping her eyes. "I just feel so sad."

"Sometimes, the best way to help yourself is to help someone else," Mrs. Akina said gently. "Now, it looks like we have customers coming. Do you want to go in the restroom and wash your face?"

As Kanani splashed cold water on her face, she thought about what her mother had said. She *was* trying to help Malana and the monk seals. But maybe

there was more she could do, especially now that she
had the late afternoons wide open.

Kanani remembered how good she had felt at
Tutu Lani's house and when she was delivering the
leis. Her mother was right—helping someone else *did*
make her feel better. That was the aloha spirit.

After closing up the shave-ice stand with Pika
that afternoon, Kanani headed out toward Tutu Lani's.
As she passed the Lees' house, she noticed that the
front door was wide open. This gave her an idea.

"Come on, Barksee, let's see how our neighbors
are doing." Kanani could hear a TV playing as she
knocked on the door. "It's Kanani," she called through
the screen door. "Can I come in?"

"Kanani? What a nice surprise," Mrs. Lee said,
coming to the door. "Come in, come in! Barksee, you
can come in, too. You're a good dog," said Mrs. Lee,
patting him approvingly as he politely followed
Kanani into the house.

"Who is it?" a gravelly voice from the next
room called out over the television noise.

"It's Kanani Akina!" Mrs. Lee answered,
leading Kanani into the front room.

Kanani looked around the tidy bungalow. On the mantle was a faded black and white wedding photo. Kanani smiled to see Mr. and Mrs. Lee looking so young and fresh. Beside it were color photos that Kanani guessed were of children and grandchildren, as well as a large portrait of the elderly couple holding a fluffy Yorkie dog the color of caramel. Kanani vaguely remembered seeing the Yorkie in their yard when she was much younger.

Mr. Lee was resting on the couch, watching golf on television. His walker was nearby. "Barksee!" Kanani called sharply as he ran up to the old man, tail wagging.

"Oh, I don't mind," Mr. Lee said as he bent down to pet Barksee. "We love dogs."

Mrs. Lee nodded. "We miss our Queenie," she said, looking at the photo of the Yorkie.

Kanani knew what it felt like to miss a pet. Each day that Jinx was gone, she felt her hopes of his return dwindle.

Kanani sat on the sofa between Mr. and Mrs. Lee and took out her digital frame. "I've got some photos I thought you might like to see," she told them and began flicking through the shots. "That's Malana, the seal pup. Isn't she cute? That's my dad's new shave-ice cart, down at the pier. And that's Pika climbing a coconut tree. What a show-off, huh?"

Mr. Lee chuckled. "When I was a boy, I could shinny up coconut palms in no time flat. Nothing like a cool drink of coconut water on a hot day!" He examined the digital frame closely. "It's like a little television for looking at pictures. What will they think of next?" he marveled.

"They're lovely photos," said Mrs. Lee as Kanani put away the frame. "Now, would you like something to drink, Kanani?"

"No, thank you—I need to get going. I'm on my way to Tutu Lani's, and I think I'll stop by Aunty Verna's on my way," Kanani replied. "But you've given me an idea—could I take some photos of you both to show Aunty Verna and Tutu Lani?"

"Why, we'd love it!" Mrs. Lee said as she scooted close to her husband.

"Barksee!" Kanani scolded as he jumped onto the sofa beside them.

"Let him stay," said Mr. Lee, putting his arm around Barksee. "This will make a nice picture!"

At Kanani's next stop, Aunty Verna filled a bowl with water for Barksee and sliced some Spam for him. Kanani noticed that her movements were slow and deliberate.

"You're going to spoil him," Kanani said as they sat on Aunty Verna's patio and listened to her wind chimes. There were more than a dozen of them, all made from shells and broken bits of raku pottery.

"I don't get many visitors to spoil," Aunty Verna said. "I love that photo of him sitting with Mr. and Mrs. Lee. They looked very happy! Will you give them my best?"

"Of course. And I can do even better than that," Kanani told Aunty Verna. "I can take your picture with Barksee and share it with them!"

Standing on the pier the next afternoon waiting for Pika to arrive, Kanani spotted Celina and Jo surfing. It hurt to watch them, but she couldn't stop looking. Last night, working on her monk-seal poster design, Kanani had almost picked up the phone to ask Celina to help her. Celina drew the daily chalkboard menu at her family's restaurant and was good at lettering. But Kanani had lost her nerve and had done the lettering on the computer instead.

"Are you spying on her?"

Kanani whipped around. "Pika!" she scolded.

"You scared me." She was tempted to swat him with the rolled-up sheet of paper she was holding, but she had worked hard on the poster and didn't want to ruin it.

Pika followed her gaze and gave a low whistle. "Man, that Jo sure knows how to surf!"

Kanani could hear the admiration in his voice. "There are lots of good surfers in Hawai'i," she said.

"Yeah, but she's really, *really* good. Not like you," Pika pointed out. "You spent more time underwater than on the board. Keala and I used to have bets on how many times you were going to wipe out—"

"Pika, just stop, okay?" Kanani pleaded. "Jim Robins and Dr. Julia Anderson are going to be here soon. Can't you at least pretend to be nice?"

"I *am* nice," Pika pouted. "Everyone says so. I should get an award for being such a nice guy."

Kanani was about to dispute this when a pretty woman with shoulder-length hair and a bright smile headed toward them, accompanied by Jim Robins. "Hi!" Kanani called to them, waving. "Dr. Anderson, have you seen Malana lately?"

"Yes, and she's doing beautifully," said the marine biologist. "Malana is exactly the size a healthy five-month-old Hawaiian monk seal should be."

"Is that the poster design?" Jim asked Kanani. "Let's see it!"

Kanani unrolled it. "I designed it on the computer," she explained. "Of course, it will be a lot bigger than this when it's printed." She held her breath as the seal experts examined her design.

"This is terrific!" Julia exclaimed. Kanani exhaled. "I'd just add a warning that the seals may bite and can cause serious injury."

"The only thing I'd change is to make the emergency number bigger," said Jim. "But this really is going to help so much. Now people will be better informed about the monk seals and will know what to do if they see one. Good job, Kanani."

"It's thanks to me the posters can get printed," Pika jumped in. "I'm more or less running the shave-ice cart. Oh, sure, I let Kanani help me out when it gets crowded, but it's mostly me. Tell them how much I've made so far," Pika said to Kanani.

Kanani rolled her eyes. "*We* have made one hundred sixty-seven dollars and fifty cents," she said proudly.

"*Both* of you have done a great job," Jim said. "On behalf of the Hawaiian monk seal, mahalo!"

Chapter 8

Tutu Lani's Honu

The following Friday, as Kanani was arranging the cupcakes in the bakery case, Mrs. Akina announced, "The Waipuna Arts and Crafts Festival is this weekend! You and Pika have done a great job with the shave-ice cart. Why don't you take a break from fund-raising until after the festival."

"I've got almost enough money for the posters," said Kanani. "Mr. Cotzee gives me a tip every time I deliver Tutu Lani's leis, and I add it to the poster fund. We're only twelve dollars from our goal!"

"That's quite an accomplishment," said her mother. "You should feel very proud."

Kanani did feel proud, but as she had watched her cash box fill up the past week, she hadn't felt the pure joy that she had expected. The poster project was something she had planned on doing with her best friend, and without Celina it just wasn't the same. And during every shift at the pier, she was keenly aware of Celina out on the water surfing and having a great time—without her.

The store was extra busy that morning, but Kanani didn't mind the work; in fact she relished it—when she was busy, there wasn't time to feel sorry for herself. Between customers, she made a list of the homemade baked goods they would need for the

weekend and then called some of their local suppliers
to place orders. "Be sure to include your coconut
meringues," she told Aunty Lea. Then she called
Aunty Aimee. "We're going to need triple the amount
of mochi you usually bring."

"Triple?" Aunty Aimee asked with delight.

"That's right," Kanani told her. "We want to be
sure we don't run out!"

At home, Mochi the goat greeted Kanani with a
series of bleats. "I missed you, too," Kanani said as
she gave Mochi a piece of bread and filled the water
bowls. Even though she had given up all hope of Jinx
returning, she kept his blue ceramic bowl full, just
in case.

After Barksee had lapped up his fill of water,
Kanani clipped on his leash. "Come on, boy, we're
going for a walk."

Their first stop was Aunty Verna's. Kanani
found her in her backyard studio. Raku vases of all
shapes and sizes lined the walls. Some were glazed
with metallic hues of green and blue and copper.
Others were a satiny black, or white with a crackled
appearance.

"You'd better stay outside, Barksee," Kanani told him. "We don't want your wagging tail to knock over a vase."

"Oh, Kanani, hello," Aunty Verna said, turning to greet her.

"I'm not interrupting you, am I?" Kanani asked.

"No, no, I was just reminiscing." Even though she was smiling, Aunty Verna sounded sad. "This will be the first year I'm not showing at the festival. It's just too much work to have a booth, and I tire so easily these days. The doctor told me to stay home this weekend and rest."

Kanani looked at a row of finished vases. They were beautiful. "We have one of your vases on display at Akina's," Kanani pointed out. "Maybe we could add a few more, and you could sell some that way."

"Oh no," Aunty Verna said. "It's your family's business—I couldn't ask you to do that."

"But we already have one of your vases from last year, and we get asked about it all the time. We could add some of your newer ones, or—hey, I know, I could take photos of them! And then if people want to buy one, we can just direct them to your studio."

"Well . . . if it's no bother," Aunty Verna said, breaking into a soft smile.

"No bother at all," Kanani assured her as she took out her camera and began taking pictures.

As Kanani made her way toward Tutu Lani's, Barksee ran ahead. Suddenly, he stopped and began barking.

"I'm coming! I'm coming!" Kanani called out. She hurried to Barksee, who was staring and barking at some dense bushes, his tail wagging. "What's in there, a mongoose?" she asked. She peered into the brush, but she couldn't see anything. "Silly dog. Come on, let's go. We're almost there."

Tutu Lani was waiting on her front porch with a pitcher of cold lemonade and two glasses on a table. "There you are," she said, holding out her hands in welcome.

The day was hot, and the cold, tart lemonade was refreshing. As she sipped, Kanani thought about the lemonade stand she'd had with Celina when they were seven, and a shaky sigh escaped her chest.

"What are you thinking of?" Tutu Lani asked.

"I didn't say anything," Kanani said.

"Not in words," the old woman replied. "Do you want to talk about it?"

Kanani told Tutu Lani that she and Celina hadn't spoken one word to each other in three weeks. "I don't know what to do," Kanani said in despair.

"What does your heart say?" asked Tutu Lani.

Kanani was silent. Over the past few weeks, every time Celina had entered her mind, she had run away from the thought, because it hurt so much. Now, as she forced herself to think about Celina and their friendship, her chest ached and tears pricked her eyes.

"My heart—feels like it's breaking," she blurted. "Oh, Tutu Lani, I just want everything back to the way it used to be, before Celina got all into surfing and Jo showed up."

The old woman nodded. "Keiki, sometimes we think things should be one way, and life offers up something . . . unexpected," she said gently. "So, you have a choice—you can turn away from it, or you can open your eyes and see where it leads." Tutu Lani patted Kanani's knee. "Let me tell you a story." The old woman settled into her rocking chair and began.

"Decades ago, when the village of Waipuna was even smaller than it is now, there was a spirited young girl who loved swimming more than anything. She would have swum day and night if she had been allowed to. The girl would go down to the beach and

swim so far out that she'd be just a speck to anyone
onshore. It was beautiful underwater. The fish were so
colorful, like sparkling gems come alive."

Kanani smiled. She knew from snorkeling how
magical the underwater world was.

"The girl's father was a fisherman," Tutu Lani
continued. "Sometimes he would anchor his small
fishing boat just a little ways offshore. One afternoon,
the girl decided to swim out and surprise him. She
knew exactly how she'd do it. She'd swim to the stern
of the boat on the side away from his fishing nets and
then climb aboard. She could just picture how aston-
ished and pleased her father would be to see her!

"The waves looked calm and the sun was
shining bright when she dove in. With strong, broad
strokes, the girl headed out toward the boat. She could
hold her breath for more than two minutes, so she
spent a lot of time under the water, coming up for air
only when it was absolutely necessary.

"On that day, it seemed as if the girl could stay
underwater for hours. She ventured out farther than
ever before. Yet each time she surfaced, the boat
seemed to be farther away, not closer. Suddenly, without warning, dark clouds gathered and the sea grew
black. When the girl surfaced for air, the waves tossed

and turned her, making her tumble as if she were caught up in a whirlwind."

Kanani took in a sharp breath. She knew what that felt like from all the times she had fallen off her surfboard.

"This wasn't an ordinary wave," Tutu Lani noted. "No, this one was different. The girl didn't know if it was a rip current, or a whirlpool, or just bad luck. She was tossed around for so long that by the time she surfaced, she could no longer see her father's boat. There was no telling how far out the currents had carried her.

"So she began to swim. After a while, the clouds parted, but the sun was so bright that it was blinding, and the girl couldn't tell which direction the shore was. She grew tired and scared. Finally, she called out, 'Someone help me, please!'"

Kanani leaned in, her eyes wide. "What happened next?"

Tutu Lani continued, "The girl was so worried that all she could think of was what would happen if she drowned. She thought about how much her family and friends would miss her. When she thought of how much she had to lose, she suddenly grew strong again.

"She began to swim with the current instead of fighting it, hoping that eventually it would take her to shore. When she was underwater, she saw something huge making its way toward her. At first, the girl was scared. She couldn't make out what it was. But as it got closer, it became clearer—it was a huge green sea turtle, a honu, swimming through the water. It was heading right at the girl.

"She panicked. Then, to her surprise, as quickly as she had filled with fear, a calm feeling washed over her like a gentle ocean wave. Instead of trying to swim away from the sea turtle, she turned and swam toward it until they were face-to-face. She put her hands over her heart to show that she was a friend.

"And do you know what the honu did?"

Kanani shook her head. Even Barksee was still.

"It slowly turned around and then looked back at her, as if to make sure the girl was following.

"At last, she caught sight of her father's boat, and she felt a sudden burst of energy. But before she swam to safety and into the arms of her father, she held her hand over her heart again, to say 'mahalo' to her friend."

"So the honu guided her to safety!" Kanani said, breathlessly.

"Yes, keiki. The honu wasn't there to harm her. The girl just didn't realize it at first." The old woman paused, and then added, "Things are not always as we think they are. When you're wondering which direction to turn, you may find answers in surprising places." Tutu Lani's eyes crinkled into a smile as she finished her story.

Kanani thought about Pika and how he had worked with her steadily over the past three weeks, selling shave ice to help the monk seals. She couldn't help feeling a little ashamed as she admitted to herself that she would never in a million years have expected Pika to be such a loyal helper—and friend.

"Tutu Lani," asked Kanani, "did you start collecting sea turtles because of that story?"

Tutu Lani's face lit up. "Yes. I have always considered sea turtles good luck. Like friends, they are always there for me."

When she got home, Kanani was delighted to find an e-mail waiting from Rachel announcing that she had gotten not one but two parakeets! One was green and one was blue, and she had named them Fred and Ginger. Then she asked about Celina.

Kanani hit "Reply" and wrote back:

Aloha, Rachel,

Please give Fred and Ginger my best. I'm so glad your mom let you get two! Now they will never be lonely.

We still haven't found Jinx and probably never will. Maybe he was lonely and joined a flock of wild chickens.

Celina and I still haven't spoken. I don't know what to say or do. Today Tutu Lani told me a story about a girl who was lost and didn't know what to do, and a green sea turtle, a honu, came to her rescue. I wish I had a honu like the girl in the story.

Aloha,

Kanani

Saturday morning Kanani got up extra early. Without Jinx to awaken her, she had started setting the red alarm clock her grandmother had given her for Christmas. Although it worked just fine, it wasn't the same as waking up to Jinx's cheerful crow, Kanani thought wistfully.

The sun was only beginning to rise as she made her way up the red dirt road. She had promised Tutu Lani that she would deliver some extra leis so that Mr. Cotzee wouldn't run out on the first day of the festival. As Kanani approached the tidy blue cottage, she thought she heard a rooster's crow. She stood still and listened. *Could it be?* Kanani held her breath, hoping to hear it again.

There it was. Kanani's heart pounded. It had to be Jinx; she'd know that crow anywhere! And it was coming from Tutu Lani's yard! She began to run.

"I told him you'd be here soon," Tutu Lani called from her porch.

"Jinx!" Kanani cried. He was perched on the railing, looking regal. Kanani scooped him up and buried her face in his feathers. He squawked and squirmed, trying to get away. "You naughty boy," she said tenderly. "Where have you been?" She turned to Tutu Lani. "You found him!"

"Actually, he found me," Tutu Lani said. "I think he's been hiding in the brush for several days. But yesterday he showed himself, and he's been hanging around ever since."

"You're right," Kanani exclaimed. "The other day, my dog was barking like crazy at something in the bushes near your house. I thought it was probably a mongoose, but I'll bet you anything it was Jinx!"

Kanani set her rooster down, and he hopped off the porch and began pecking around the garden. "He likes it here," the old woman said as she looked fondly at him. "My berries are so juicy and ripe that they fall to the ground, and Jinx has been feasting on them. I think Sue is in love with him—and the feeling appears to be mutual."

Kanani looked over at Sue, who was following Jinx around. "They make a nice couple," she quipped. It was so wonderful to see her rooster again.

"Jinx," Tutu Lani called, throwing a handful of corn on the ground. "Come, say aloha."

Kanani smiled. Poor Tutu Lani had no idea how difficult her rooster was. Jinx never obeyed anyone's commands. When he strutted over to Tutu Lani and let her pick him up without protesting, Kanani was shocked.

"He's a good rooster," Tutu Lani said as she gazed at him. "He's good company, too."

"Jinx?" Kanani couldn't believe how well he was behaving. He had never once come to her when she called him. Instead, it seemed as if she was always chasing him around the backyard, and he always acted as if he had somewhere better to be.

She had worried for weeks about Jinx, and now here he was. It would be easy, Kanani reflected, to just pick him up and take him home. But she couldn't help seeing that Tutu Lani and Jinx seemed to have a special rapport. And with Sue clucking contentedly nearby, they looked like a family.

"You know," Kanani began, "Jinx really seems to love it here, and no wonder—you have so many delicious fruits and berries. And you said he and Sue are in love. So maybe," she said, trying not to stumble over her words, "maybe he should stay with you."

Tutu Lani shook her head. "Oh no, keiki, Jinx is your rooster."

Kanani shook her head. "Not really, not any longer. He left my yard and came to yours. And he seems at home here. It would make me happy to know that he was with you and Sue." Kanani felt a little ache in her chest, but she knew in her heart that although Jinx had grown up with her, he had come home to Tutu Lani.

Slowly, a smile lit up the old woman's face. "All right then, he can stay—as long as you promise to visit us often!"

Kanani knew that would be an easy promise to keep. As her rooster settled in Tutu Lani's lap, Kanani was finally able to let go of a long sigh that she felt she'd been holding inside ever since Jinx first went missing. She reached into her pocket for her camera. "Do you mind if I take some pictures of the two of you?" she asked.

Tutu Lani's eyes crinkled into a broad smile. "Not at all. Perhaps I'll have a new career as a fashion model!"

The quiet town of Waipuna was abuzz. The festival was in full swing, and the surf competition had been under way since early that morning.

"Aloha and welcome to Akina's!" Kanani felt as if she had said, "Aloha and welcome to Akina's" a thousand times that morning, but she didn't mind. She loved seeing the store bustling with happy customers.

"Honey, you've been working so hard, why don't you take a break and go check out the arts and crafts?" Mrs. Akina suggested. "Don't forget to select something special for the store."

Kanani looked over at a couple who were admiring her photos of Aunty Verna's raku pottery. "The artist's studio is just up the road," she told them.

Kanani stepped outside onto Koa Street. The town had been completely transformed. Instead of cars in the streets, there were rows of colorful booths, each one crammed full of one-of-a-kind treasures that beckoned with the promise of surprise and delight: oil paintings of the Kaua'i shoreline at sunset, sleek sculptures of dolphins, stained-glass kaleidoscopes, shell wind chimes, and every sort of jewelry—colorful sea-glass necklaces, bracelets woven from the sturdy leaves of the hala tree, and thick strands of lustrous *kukui* nuts.

In past years, Kanani and Celina had always played a private game at the festival: at every booth, they each tried to guess what the other one's favorite piece was. Kanani sighed, remembering. It wasn't a game you could play alone.

Instead, she pulled out her camera and took pictures of her favorite pieces. If Aunty Verna and the

Lees and Tutu Lani couldn't come to the festival, she would bring the festival to them!

While Kanani was admiring some interesting vases made from gourds, Pika ran up. "Did you hear?" he asked breathlessly. "Seth is in the finals for the championship trophy tomorrow!"

"That's wonderful!" Kanani exclaimed.

"I didn't know that Celina was in the tournament, too," Pika said. "Did you?"

Kanani was stunned. This was news to her.

"The girls' competition is almost over," he went on. "So if you want to watch, you'd better hurry!"

Kanani nodded, still shocked from the news. "I—I'm going right now."

Slowly, Kanani headed toward the beach. But with each step, she began to go faster, her thoughts tumbling over each other like waves. When had Celina decided to enter the competition? This was a big deal for Celina, Kanani knew. Yet Celina had said nothing to her about it.

As Kanani got closer, she could hear the roar of the spectators. She quickened her pace when the announcer declared, "And now the last surfer in Beginning Junior Girls—Celina de la Cruz!"

Kanani wove through the crowd as fast as she

could, her heart pounding. Even though the summer had not gone exactly as they had planned, Celina was still her friend—this her heart was telling her loudly. Surfing wasn't just something Celina did for fun; she was serious about it. Kanani desperately wanted to be there for her friend's first competition, but she couldn't break through the crowd to get to the beach.

"And that ends the Junior Girls Competition," the announcer said. Kanani couldn't believe it. She had missed seeing Celina compete.

The announcer continued. "Here are the results: Third place in the Beginning Junior Girls category, Quinn Littman! Second place, Celina de la Cruz!"

Kanani felt a burst of energy and pushed her way to the stage. "Celina!" she yelled, jumping up and down to get her attention. "Celina!" But she was drowned out by the announcer's voice.

"And first place goes to . . . Jo Amoy!"

As Jo waved to the crowd, Celina hugged her, and the two girls held up their trophies. Kanani had never seen Celina look as happy as she did sharing the spotlight with Jo.

Although there were hundreds of people around her, Kanani suddenly felt utterly alone. Turning away, she drifted back toward the festival. The crowds reminded her of a day last year when a carnival had come to the island. She and Celina had ridden the Tilt-a-Whirl four times. Kanani felt as if she were on the ride again, only this time it was her emotions whirling dizzily—and Celina wasn't there beside her.

Kanani wandered from booth to booth, hoping that the arts and crafts would distract her from thinking about Celina and Jo.

"That's a juniper bonsai," said a friendly Chinese man with white hair. "It's more than seventy-five years old. The older bonsai is, the more beautiful and valuable it becomes," he told her.

Seventy-five years old! That was almost as old as Tutu Lani. Kanani peered at the tiny juniper. It was knarled and twisty, with tiny blue-green needles. The bonsai man was right—it was beautiful.

The next booth had glorious underwater photographs. Kanani could not believe how sharp and clear the images were. Colorful coral reefs, illuminated jellyfish, jet-black stingrays—the photos instantly transported her below the surface of the ocean where the sea came alive. "Your photos are amazing," she told the man in the booth. "They make me feel as if I'm right there under the water, snorkeling!"

The man laughed. "I can't take credit for what

the ocean has to offer, but I try to do it justice." The man looked vaguely familiar, Kanani thought. Had she seen him at the festival last year? Something about his eyes—

"Daddy! Daddy, look!" a girl called, and the man broke into a huge grin. "Jo!" he called out. "You won a trophy!"

Kanani looked up. It was Jo—Jo the surfer, Celina's new friend and Kanani's replacement. *I have to get out of here,* Kanani thought urgently. But how could she leave without being obvious? She turned and pretended to be fascinated by the photos.

"Kanani?" Jo asked. "Kanani, is that you?"

"Oh, hi," Kanani stammered. She looked at Jo's big trophy and winced. "Congratulations."

"Thanks," Jo replied. "Celina got a trophy, too! She placed second, which is awesome for her first competition."

Hearing Celina's name, Kanani felt a lump in her throat. She forced a smile and said, "Wow, that is great. That's wonderful . . . for both of you."

"Daddy," Jo said, turning to her father, "this is Kanani, the girl I told you about."

She told her father about me? Kanani wondered.

The man in the booth smiled. "Nice to meet

you, Kanani," he said. "I'm Marcus Amoy."

Suddenly it all made sense. Kanani had heard of Marcus Amoy, the famous underwater photographer, and she knew that Jo's father was exhibiting in the festival. Jo's emerald green eyes were just like her father's—that was why he looked familiar.

"My daughter tells me that you're a photographer, too," Mr. Amoy said.

Kanani blushed. How would Jo know that she liked taking pictures? "It's just a hobby," she said. "I'm not that good at it." She felt a little embarrassed to be called a photographer in front of Marcus Amoy.

"That's not what I hear," replied Jo. "Celina says you're great. She showed me some of your photos that she has framed in her room. And she's right—you *are* talented." Jo grinned. "I should know, right?"

Is this true? Kanani wondered. Did Celina and Jo both think she was good at photography?

"Celina really admires your talent. She wishes she was artistic like you," Jo went on. "She says her photos are always blurry, or she accidentally cuts people's heads off." Kanani couldn't help smiling. "Celina says you're a great hula dancer, too. She talks about you so much," Jo continued, "I feel like we're already friends."

The Festival

As Jo spoke, Kanani felt shame wash over her. This girl was really nice, yet Kanani had never even given her a chance.

Maybe there was still time. "Have you always surfed?" Kanani asked.

Jo let out a laugh. "I wish! No, I tried karate, and soccer, and even diving, but I wasn't very good at any of them. Then my cousin took me surfing, and I loved it."

"Maybe the three of us could get together," Kanani suggested.

Jo smiled. "That would be awesome," she said. "We're here for a few more days, aren't we, Dad?"

Mr. Amoy nodded. "That's right. We leave on Tuesday."

"I just love your photographs," Kanani told Jo's father.

"Why don't you bring some of yours by later?" Mr. Amoy suggested. "I'd like to see them."

"You would?" The thought of showing her snapshots to a professional, an artist like Mr. Amoy, made Kanani feel shy, but it was also sort of exciting. "Okay, I'll bring them by tomorrow." She turned to go.

"Bye, Kanani!" called Jo.

"Bye, Jo!" Smiling, Kanani waved at her.

On Sunday morning, Kanani wasn't the only one up at sunrise. "I heard you're in the finals today," she said to Seth as he waxed his board. She admired the row of colorful surfboards leaning against the yellow beach cottage. Anyone would know that a family of surfers lived there.

Seth flashed a nervous grin. "Some big names are in the competition, so I'm just going to give it my best, and whatever happens, happens."

The screen door opened. "Seth, who are you talking to?" Celina asked. Suddenly she saw Kanani and stopped in the doorway.

"Hi, Celina," Kanani said shyly.

"Oh, hi," Celina replied, her voice cautious.

Seth grabbed his board. "See you guys at the beach," he said.

Both girls wished him luck, but neither moved. They just stared at each other.

Finally Kanani spoke. "Congratulations on winning second place."

Celina shrugged. "I got lucky."

Kanani shook her head. "No—you worked very hard for that trophy. You're a great surfer."

"You could be great, too," said Celina. "It just takes practice."

Kanani took a deep breath. "Celina, I'm in total awe of what you can do, and Jo, too. I mean, you two can surf all day and still want to surf more. Me? Well, I tried, I really did, but I'm not a natural like you and Seth and Jo, and I just don't enjoy it enough to do all the practicing it would take to get better. I hope you're not too disappointed with me."

Celina was speechless for a long moment, and Kanani's heart sank. She knew she had let her friend down.

At last, Celina spoke. "Oh no," she said softly. "Kanani, I am so sorry. I just realized how much I've been pressuring you to surf. I guess I was so caught up with it that I assumed you'd feel the same way."

Kanani exhaled. "It's not just you. It was me, too. I was so excited about raising money to help the monk seals that I took for granted that you'd feel the same way. When I figured out that you'd rather surf, I got upset and hurt. But even though we like to do different things, I still really, really hope we can be best friends. I've missed you so much—"

"I've missed you, too," Celina said quietly.

"And—I was jealous of Jo," Kanani admitted. "She's so good at surfing, and the two of you looked like you were having so much fun together." Kanani hung her head. "It wasn't fair to her—to either of you. I should have given her a chance."

"We do have a lot of fun, but there's no reason for you to be jealous," Celina assured her. "Still, I can understand why you felt that way. I mean, that's sort of how I felt about Rachel."

"Really?" Kanani was shocked. "You were jealous of my cousin?"

"Well, sure. Instead of doing stuff with me, you were with Rachel for a month. But after I got to know her, I realized that you were being a really good friend to her. That was one of the reasons I kept Jo company—because that's what *you* would have done for a girl who was in a new place without any friends, like you did for Rachel." Celina sighed. "Jo's great and really nice—but, Kanani, you're the one who's my best friend." She hesitated for a moment and then added, "You know, I'm actually sort of relieved to know that you don't like surfing."

"You are?" asked Kanani.

"Yes—because I thought it was me you were trying to avoid. Now I know it was just *surfing* you wanted to get away from!"

"Well, at least *you* got to spend time with a nice girl like Jo when you were surfing. *I* had to sell shave ice with *Pika!*" Kanani laughed, and Celina joined her. "Actually, though, he wasn't so bad," she admitted. "But he's no Celina de la Cruz!"

With the second day of the festival in full swing, Akina's Shave Ice and Sweet Treats overflowed with customers. All morning the shave ice machine whirred nonstop, and Kanani expertly poured the colorful syrups onto huge cones of powdery ice.

"Have you chosen a new art piece for the store yet?" Mr. Akina asked.

"I think so," Kanani said as she handed an orange, papaya, and grape shave ice to a teenage boy. He held it high in the air like a trophy, and his friends applauded.

"The festival ends in a couple of hours," Kanani's father told her. "Your mother and I have things under control here—you go on and enjoy the festival."

This time Kanani headed straight to Mr. Amoy's booth. One photo in particular had caught her eye—a large framed image of a honu swimming underwater, looking straight at the viewer. Its face looked kind and friendly. Kanani imagined being the girl in Tutu Lani's story and following the honu to safety.

"How much is this one?" she asked Mr. Amoy.

"That one's two hundred and fifty dollars," Mr. Amoy replied.

"Oh," Kanani said. She knew that was beyond her parents' budget.

"I have a smaller unframed print that I could sell you for forty dollars," Mr. Amoy added. "By the way, did you bring your photos?"

Kanani nodded. Nervously, she held up her digital-photo frame and scrolled through the pictures as Mr. Amoy studied her photos.

"You know," Mr. Amoy said at last, "you have quite a gift."

"It was from my cousin Rachel," Kanani said.

Mr. Amoy chuckled. "No, I mean you have natural talent—you have *an eye*, as they say in the photography business." He scrolled through the photos and stopped on the one of Tutu Lani holding Jinx. Her wrinkled hands contrasted with the rooster's sleek feathers. "I love this one," he said. "The different textures are wonderful, and the expression on the woman's face speaks volumes. You know, the old woman and the proud rooster make a rather unexpected pair, but that makes the picture interesting—and you can sure tell that they belong together."

Kanani looked at her photo. Mr. Amoy was right—Tutu Lani and Jinx did belong together, and somehow her photo had captured that.

"Will you sell me a copy of this photo?" Mr. Amoy asked.

Kanani was speechless. The great Marcus Amoy wanted to buy one of her photos? "Sure . . . yes, okay," she stammered.

"Great!" he said. "What do you charge?"

"I have no idea," Kanani admitted. "How about a dollar?"

"How about ten dollars?" Mr. Amoy suggested.

Ten dollars? If she added it to the money she had already raised, she'd need only two more dollars to get the monk seal posters printed.

"How about twelve dollars?" Kanani blurted.

Mr. Amoy let out a loud laugh. "You're an artist *and* a businesswoman," he said, reaching out to shake her hand. "It's a deal!"

Kanani held her breath as her parents studied her selection. Finally, Mrs. Akina exclaimed, "I love it!"

Kanani let out a sigh of relief. The honu photo

was a hit, and it looked perfect mounted on the wall of the store next to the article about Malana.

She smiled to herself. Her parents didn't know it, but the photo had a secret personal meaning to her. It would be a daily reminder of Tutu Lani's wise advice to be open to the unexpected and to look for friends in surprising places.

"The honu has so much character," her father said, "and the ocean looks so inviting—"

The ocean! Kanani looked at the clock. "Gotta go—Seth's surfing finals are about to start!" she called as she ran out of the store. This time she was determined not to be late.

Celina and Jo were waiting for her near the lifeguard station. "I didn't miss it, did I?" Kanani asked.

"Seth is the second-to-last surfer," Celina told her. "Come on!"

Together, the three girls ran down to the beach to cheer Seth on.

On the soft white sand of the beach at 'Olino Cove, Kanani stood with her board, looking out at the sparkling water. The Waipuna Arts and Crafts Festival had been over for a week, but Kanani still felt festive. There were so many things to celebrate: Seth had nailed his last wave and clinched the championship, Kanani's elderly friends had loved looking at her photos of the festival, and Aunty Verna had sold six vases. And the thing that lifted Kanani's heart the highest of all—renewing her friendship with Celina.

"Ready?"

Kanani turned. Celina was there with her own board and paddle.

"Ready!" Kanani answered, and the girls carried their paddleboards to the water.

The paddleboards were longer than surfboards and shaped differently. While Seth sat nearby on his surfboard, keeping an eye on them, Kanani felt her body relax as she kneeled on her board and navigated across the glassy surface of the ocean. The water in 'Olino Cove was calm, with gentle ripples. Flashes of yellow bolted beneath her as a school of fish flitted through the turquoise water. Kanani rose to her feet and stood on her board, balancing easily as she paddled out from shore. Without big waves to worry about, she had no fear of falling. She waved to Seth, and he waved back.

Off in the distance, Kanani spotted two surfers, and for a moment, she felt a tinge of regret. She glanced at Celina. "I hope this isn't too boring for you," she said, half playfully but half wondering what Celina really thought.

"Are you kidding?" said Celina. "I love paddle-boarding—it's so relaxing. And it's great to just chill out with your best friend."

Kanani grinned and raised her hand in the shaka sign, and Celina gave her a shaka in reply.

A few days later, the girls stood admiring the monk seal poster in the window of Akina's Shave Ice and Sweet Treats. "It looks great," Celina said.

"The posters came out even better than I had hoped," Kanani agreed as she bit into her shave ice. Looking at the big glossy poster in the window, she couldn't help feeling proud. No one who came into Akina's could miss it!

"I sent one to Rachel, too," she told Celina.

On the back of Rachel's poster, Kanani had written a note:

Best Friends

Aloha, Rachel,

Here's something unique for your new room. In all of New York, no one else has a poster like this!

I saw Malana today at the cove. She's come a long way since we found her stranded on the beach.

I think we all have.

Love always,

Kanani

P.S. Celina and I are still best friends. I should never have doubted her.

"Principal Ikeda says that we can put up a poster in each classroom," Kanani told Celina.

"We'll put up two at Waipuna Kitchen," Celina said. "One inside the restaurant for people to see while they're eating, and one in the window for people to see when they pass by."

"That's a great idea!" Kanani paused and then asked, "Do you want to help me put them up around town? If you're too busy, that's okay—no problem." She grinned mischievously. "I could probably get Pika to help me."

Celina pretended to look insulted. "Great! So now I've been replaced by Pika?"

Kanani laughed. "Not a chance! Pika's all right,

but like I said, he's no Celina de la Cruz. Here, take these." She handed her best friend an armload of posters and then scooped up a pile herself. "Well, what are we waiting for?" Kanani asked. "Let's get started!"

Glossary of Hawaiian Words

aloha *(ah-LO-hah)*—hello, good-bye, love, compassion

honu *(hoh-NOO)*—a green sea turtle

keiki *(KAY-kee)*—child

kukui *(koo-KOO-ee)*—a tree with large, smooth nuts

mahalo *(mah-HAH-lo)*—thank you

mu'umu'u *(MOO-moo)*—a long, loose dress that is a
   traditional Hawaiian garment for women

pika *(PEE-kah)*—rock or stone

shaka *(SHAH-kah)*—a hand gesture that can mean "hi,"
   "see you later," "everything's cool," or "all right!"

Letter from American Girl

Dear Readers,

   Kanani discovered that helping others felt good and made her happy. Here are the stories of six real girls who have offered a helping hand to others. Each of these girls learned that by offering small gifts and services, they made a *big* difference in people's lives. One girl helped others preserve beautiful memories for the future, and other girls worked to ensure health and happiness for people who could use a friendly smile. Though their projects took a lot of hard work, each big-hearted helper soon discovered that her efforts were well worth the joy they brought to others.

   We hope you are inspired by these real girls and their real stories. There are many ways to help, big and small. With creativity and determination, you, too, can make a difference!

   Your friends at American Girl

PHOTO FRIENDLY

Francesca L. got her own camera when she was eight years old, and she loved taking photos. A few years ago, when she asked to see photos of her grandmother as a girl, Francesca was surprised to learn that her grandmother had only one photo from her own childhood. That's when Francesca got an idea—she'd take photos of people who didn't usually get their photos taken. She wanted them to have photos to show their own grandchildren one day.

Francesca's mom helped her get in touch with a local homeless shelter, and the Florida girl set to work. "When I got there, all of the little children were running around, screaming, "Take my picture! Take my picture!" remembers Francesca. She took almost 150 photos of kids and their families. She then developed all of the photos and put them into small albums for the families to keep.

The people at the shelter were thrilled to get the albums, and one mom even cried with happiness, Francesca says. "I feel really good about what I did, and I hope that they will have these pictures to treasure until they grow old."

Francesca is now 14 and has continued to take pictures at the homeless shelter every Mother's Day for the past four years. She now has a portable photo printer that allows her to print photos on the spot!

HAIR HEROINE

Haley T. wanted to give someone a gift. She'd learned about a program that collected human hair to make wigs. The wigs went to kids who had lost their own hair through illness. It took the 11-year-old Georgia girl a year and four months to grow nearly a foot of hair, and she was excited to give it to someone who needed it.

Not that it was entirely easy. "I was really nervous," Haley remembers. "When it was the big day, I started thinking that maybe I didn't want to do this." But the hairstylist worked quickly. She separated Haley's hair into sections, and then *snip, snip!*—the hair was gone in an instant.

"I felt so great that I made a difference," Haley says, knowing that her hair went to a child who would appreciate it. "And I love my new hairdo now!"

SEW SPECIAL

Andrea F. loves to sew. One day during a visit to a fabric store, the Canadian girl got an idea to sew mini beanbags to give to patients at the children's hospital where her dad works. Andrea's mom suggested that she make something that could be washed easily, so Andrea chose to make pillowcases instead. She picked out fabric with a wild animal print and got to work.

Andrea sewed a pile of pillowcases, and when they were all finished, her dad took her to the children's hospital to drop them off. "It seemed scary at first, and I was nervous," Andrea remembers. "But the nurses were nice. And when we got home, I was really happy to have done something nice for those kids."

Andrea continues to sew pillowcases for the children's hospital, and she has taken on other service activities as well. Last year, Andrea's family took a trip to South Africa, where they visited an orphanage outside of Cape Town. When they returned home, Andrea couldn't stop thinking about her time at the orphanage. On her tenth birthday, she asked her friends and family to donate money to the orphanage instead of buying her gifts. This inspired her music teacher to ask for donations at an end-of-the-year recital. In all, Andrea and her peers were able to donate $600 to the orphanage.

BLIZZARD BUDDY

Lindsey M. lives in the mountains of Colorado, where snowstorms can make driving impossible. Lindsey, age 11, knew that some of her elderly or disabled neighbors relied on meals delivered by volunteer drivers. If a bad snowstorm hit and drivers couldn't get through, some people might have to go without food. So a few years ago, Lindsey came up with a way to help: she decided to make up boxes of emergency food for her elderly neighbors.

After writing to local organizations to raise money, Lindsey collected shoeboxes and then hit the grocery store with her mom. They bought canned peaches, beef stew, tuna, sausages, and tomato juice, as well as crackers, cookies, and peppermints. Lindsey filled, taped, labeled, and delivered nearly 40 Blizzard Boxes, containing several meals each, to folks who otherwise might have had to wait out a snowstorm without much to eat. "When I realized how much of a difference I made, it made me feel really good," Lindsey says.

Today, Lindsey continues to extend a helping hand to others in need. She and a friend recently held a baby shower for a center that helps pregnant mothers in need of extra help and resources. Lindsay has also collected all the money she has received from her allowance, Christmas, and her birthday to sponsor three children in need. She writes letters to the children and sends them little gifts, like stickers and coloring books.

GOLDEN GIRL

Ellen B. and her friends got to talking when they learned of their beloved school custodian's lifelong dream. "We read in our school paper that Mr. Venable has nine kids and a dog named Blackie, and that he has always dreamed of visiting the Golden Gate Bridge," Ellen remembers.

The North Carolina girls decided to try to make Mr. Venable's dream come true. Ellen, age 11, wrote to the school superintendent, asking if she and her friends could raise money to send their hardworking custodian and his wife on a trip to San Francisco, California, to see the Golden Gate Bridge. Permission was granted, and the girls worked with their parents, teachers, and churches to raise about $2,000.

The school principal helped to make reservations for the airplane and hotel, and Mr. Venable had tears in his eyes when he was presented with the tickets at a school assembly. "I'm so proud to have helped make Mr. Venable's wish come true," said Ellen. "He was touched that we cared about him."

SNEAKER SEEKER

When Emily L. runs, she feels free. But in other parts of the world, running can give girls actual freedom. Emily learned about girls in Ethiopia (a country in Africa) who joined running programs that allowed them to attend school and have better lives. When Emily found out that some girls couldn't run—or go to school—because they didn't have running shoes, she sprinted into action, collecting gently used shoes to donate to girls in need.

"I made posters and decorated collection boxes," says Emily, who also spoke to community groups about her cause. In all, Emily collected more than 200 pairs of shoes. The 10-year-old Virginia girl and her family then piled the shoes in the car and delivered them to an organization that would clean and ship the shoes to Africa.

"I'll keep on collecting shoes," says Emily, "so that more girls in Ethiopia can experience the freedom of running."

Emily continues to help kids closer to home through her church and Girl Scouts. Recently she led an outdoor program for fourth graders, which taught them to relieve stress through yoga and other relaxing activities in a nearby park.

Lisa Yee has wanted to be an author since she was 10 years old. "I thought it would be cool," she said, "but I never guessed that it could be this exciting!" Lisa loves Hawai'i and visits as often as she can. Before writing *Aloha, Kanani* and *Good Job, Kanani*, Lisa returned to the islands and took surfing lessons and paddle-board lessons. She also went snorkeling and saw a Hawaiian monk seal on the beach. Most importantly, she ate dozens of shave ice cones—sometimes six a day—all in the name of research! Lisa lives in South Pasadena, California, with her daughter, son, husband, and a Labradoodle dog who likes to chew on books.

You can learn more about Lisa at www.lisayee.com.